TEN
TIMES
BETTER

POEMS AND TEXT BY RICHARD MICHELSON
PAINTINGS BY LEONARD BASKIN

MARSHALL CAVENDISH · NEW YORK

Text copyright © 2000 by Richard Michelson
Illustrations copyright © 2000 by Leonard Baskin
All rights reserved
Marshall Cavendish, 99 White Plains Road, Tarrytown, New York 10951

Michelson, Richard
Ten times better / by Richard Michelson, illustrated by Leonard Baskin
p. cm.
Summary: Descriptions of different animals highlight the numbers from one to ten and their multiples of ten,
such as a sloth having three toes while a centipede has thirty feet.
ISBN 0-7614-5070-X
1. Ten (The number)—Juvenile literature. 2. Multiplication—Juvenile literature. 3. Animals—Juvenile literature.
[1. Counting. 2. Multiplication. 3. Animals.] I. Title. II. Illustrator.
00-026183
Dewey decimal number on file.

The text of this book is set in Galliard.
The paintings are watercolors.
Printed in China
First edition

3   5   6   4

For Jen, my BETTER half, TIMES TEN
—R.M.

For Lucien, with love
—L.B.

My favorite number's number ONE.

When I was ONE, I weighed ONE ton.

When I get hot, my ONE big schnoz'll

double as a shower nozzle.

Big nose? Big deal. I'm TEN times wetter

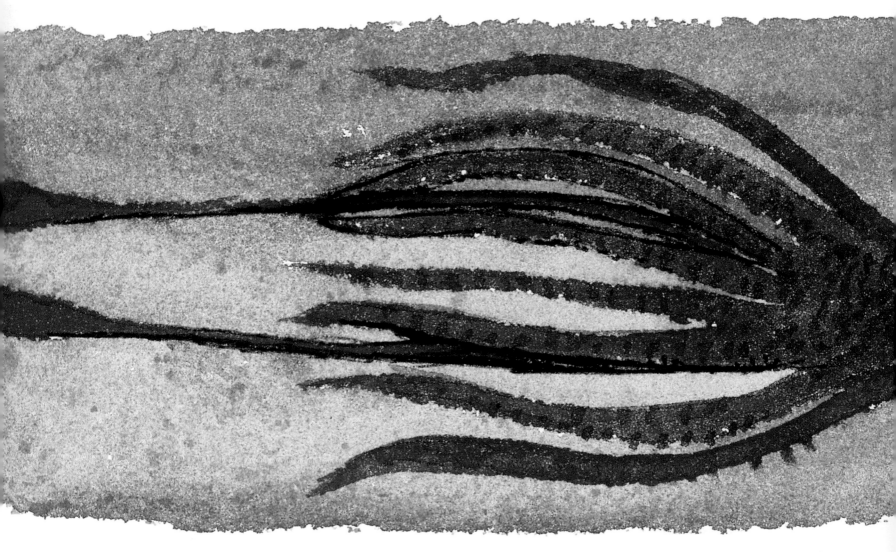

for cleaning and counting. It's much more fun

TEN tentacles are TEN TIMES BETTER

to times by ten, than add by one.

8

The coolest number's TWO. It's true!

I have TWO eyes, TWO ears — like you.

But I have extras that you lack,

TWO hairy bumps on my bactrian back.

Two bumps? Too bad. Ladies and gentry
like me TEN TIMES BETTER. TWENTY
feathers spike out from my tail.
You can't upstage a sage grouse male.

9

I know the nicest number's THREE.

Mom says I'm slow. She flatters me.

I'm lazy, lax, and proud of both.

That's praise if you're a THREE-toed sloth.

Just three? Dear me. The centipede

is TEN TIMES BETTER. Built for speed,

our THIRTY feet are quite a plus.

We're fast — if no one steps on us.

I'm sure the foremost number's FOUR.
For handsome tusks, the wild boar
is tops, though some might also choose a
warthog or male babirusa.

Four's fun for sure. But if you're warty,
more is better. I have FORTY.
That's why princesses like frogs
TEN TIMES BETTER than warthogs.

13

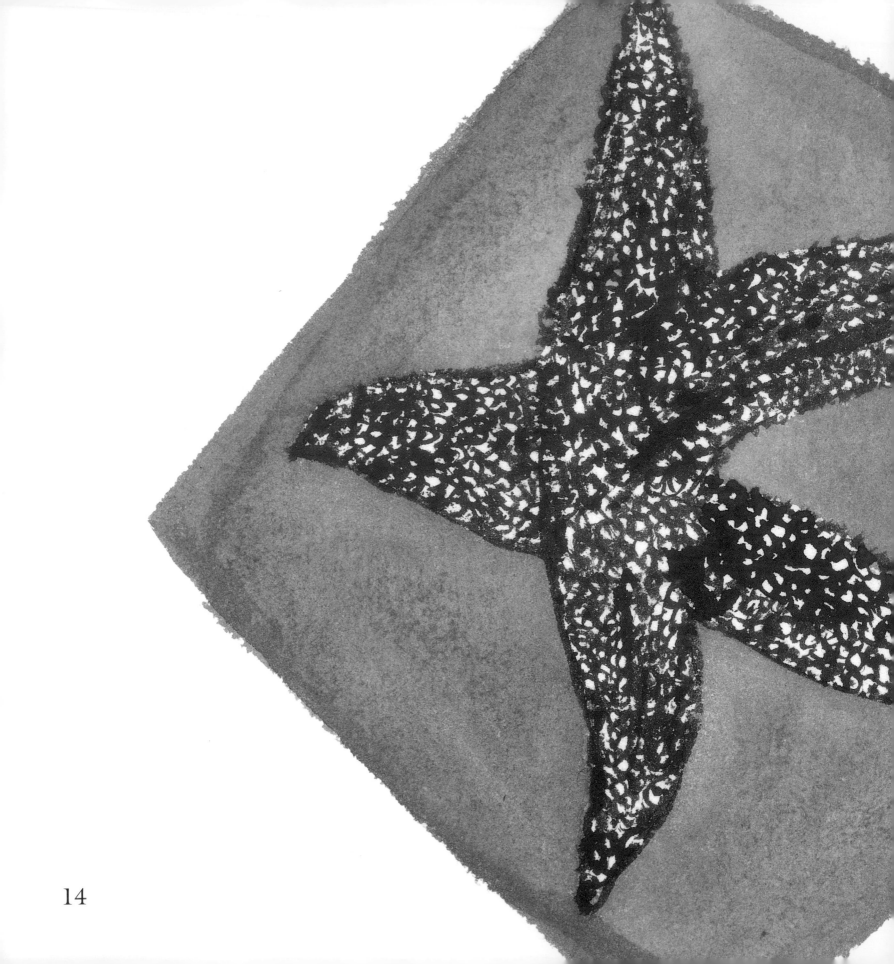

I say FIVE'S the hippest number.

It's true I can't hiphop or rhumba,

can't sing, can't jive, can't play guitar.

But count my arms — I'm still a star.

You wish. Goldfish are rich *and* famous.
We hate to brag, but who can blame us.
We're TEN TIMES BETTER. Sure, five's nifty,
but cool fish swim in schools of FIFTY.

Who goes outside without their pants
and has SIX legs? You guessed it: ants.
We've never learned arithmetic,
but SIX is better. That's our pick.

Fiddlesticks! Six, the best? Poppycock!
You want TEN TIMES BETTER? Dial a croc.
I have SIXTY teeth. I'm a great masticator.
(That means I chew first, and ask questions later.)

My mask makes me look like a bandit in jail,

but my number's heavenly—count on my tail.

I have SEVEN halos, that's how I perceive it.

Raccoons into stealing? Don't you believe it!

Seven? Good heavens! So what? Count my spots.

I'm TEN TIMES BETTER. Giraffes have...well, lots.

Me, I have SEVENTY just on my neck.

Heck, you can count them yourself. C'mon check.

What number's best? There can be no debate—
tarantulas know that the greatest is EIGHT.
I'll tell you why if you look in my eyes.
Come close...can't see you...come closer. Surprise!

23

You're hairy and scary, but you must be blind. See,
I have EIGHTY eyes, and that's just behind me.
That's TEN TIMES BETTER. I hate to sound snooty,
but even your mom wouldn't call you a beauty.

I find no number is finer than NINE.

Here on my back is a NINE-band design.

I know I'm not cute in this suit. I'm no charmer,
but I'm safer in here than a knight in full armor.

Nine's fine, no doubt for you small scaly types,
but I'm TEN TIMES BETTER. I have NINETY stripes.
I ponder one question all day and all night:
whether they're black, or whether they're white.

29

The number that pleases most all chimpanzees is
TEN! Simply put, TENS are all masterpieces.
Why else would we have TEN toes and TEN fingers?
Even humans agree, TENS are humdingers.

31

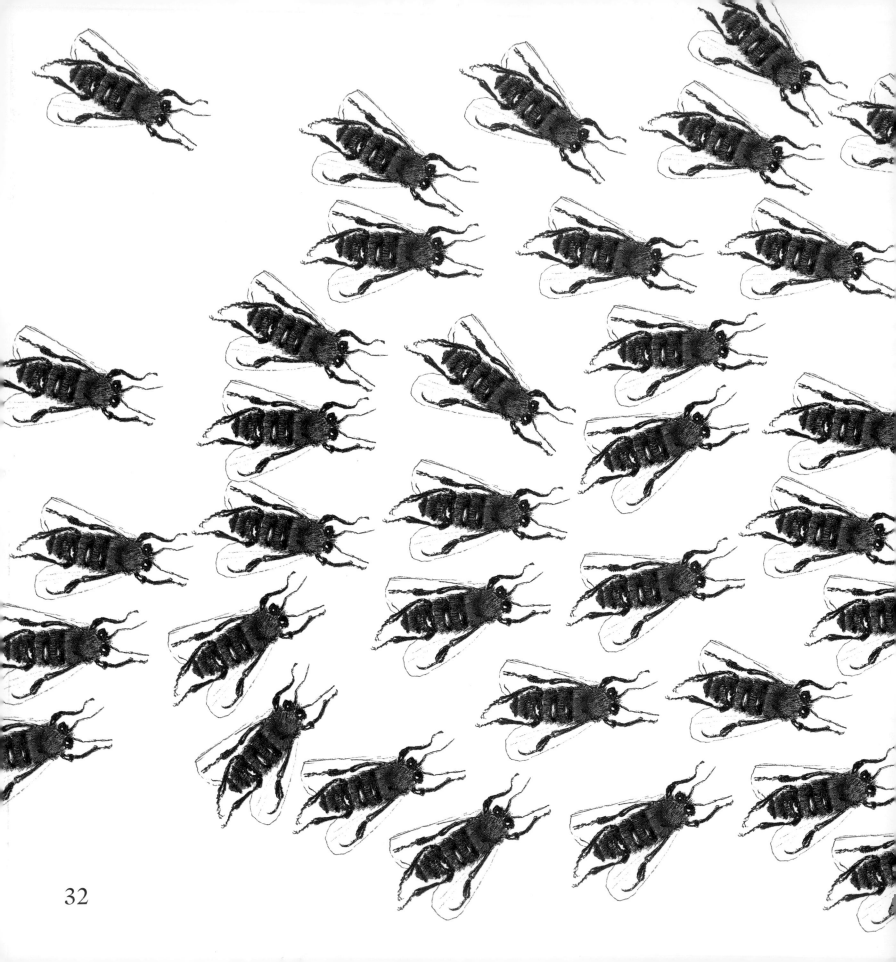

Ten's necessary. All numbers are needed

but we humble bumble bees aren't conceited.

Our hive has ONE HUNDRED, but without each ONE,

you'd have two big ZEROS, which add up to none.

No one's TEN TIMES BETTER, but, may we suggest,

if we *count* on each other, we'll all *bee* our best.

33

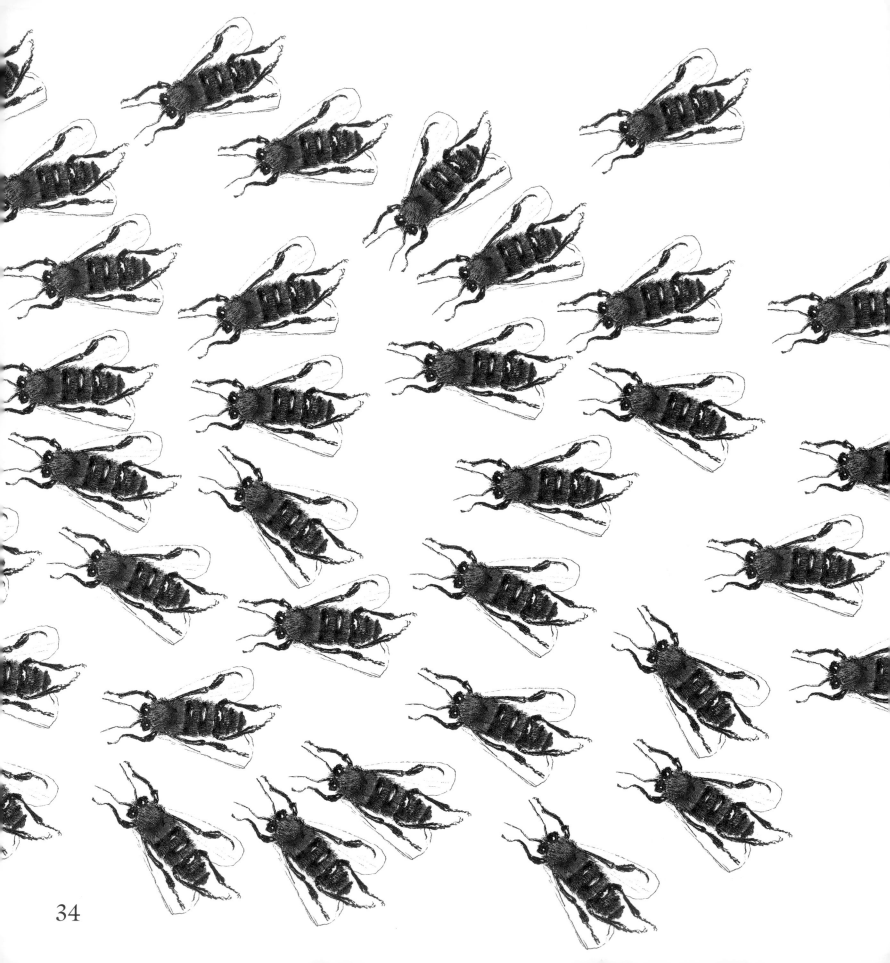

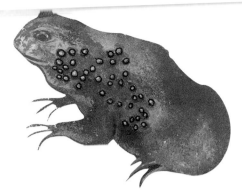

FROG

Most frogs have smooth skin, but a few have warty backs. A frog's skin will stretch as it grows, until it splits and falls off (a new skin grows under the old.) The frog will eat its original skin for protein.

Frogs would make great Olympic long jumpers. Most people can jump as far as they are tall, but a frog can jump TEN TIMES FARTHER. A six foot tall person can jump about six feet. If a frog were six feet tall, how far could it leap?

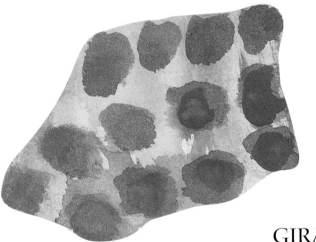

GIRAFFE

Giraffes are the tallest land animals. Baby giraffes are over six feet tall when they are born.
Every giraffe's neck has a unique pattern of spots. Their necks alone grow taller than the tallest person.

A baby giraffe can stand on its own ten minutes after birth and it can run within ten hours. Even a small baby giraffe is TEN TIMES HEAVIER than a huge human baby. If that baby weighs eleven pounds at birth (most weigh seven to eight pounds), how much might a small baby giraffe weigh?

GOLDFISH

Animals that have backbones are called vertebrates. Fish were the first vertebrates; before frogs, snakes, birds, or people. Goldfish are about ¼ inch when they are born, less than the length of a pencil eraser. How big they grow depends on their environment and whether they have good food and clean water.

A goldfish kept in a small crowded bowl might grow to be two inches. Another goldfish swimming in a big pond could grow TEN TIMES LONGER. How long would this goldfish grow to be?

PEACOCK

When the peacock displays his train feathers in a shimmering fan, he is the most magnificent of birds. His feathers reflect colors the way the surface of a soap bubble does. Like hair, feathers are not living, so they contain no blood vessels and they are very light.

Feathers are TEN TIMES LIGHTER than skin which is filled with blood vessels. A peacock's feathers weigh about three pounds. If feathers were filled with blood vessels, how many pounds would a peacock drag around all day?

Answers can be found on page 40.

RACCOON

With bands of black hair around their eyes creating "bandit masks," raccoons really are nighttime raiders. They steal scraps from trash cans and food from refrigerators, often working together; one raccoon passing food out an open window to another. They are expert at using their paws to pry open lids and doors. They can even untie knots.

Sometimes, raccoons jump out in front of cars during their escape, although most make a clean getaway. TEN TIMES MORE squirrels are run over every summer than raccoons. If, in your town, eight raccoons are killed by cars, how many squirrels are likely to have lost their lives?

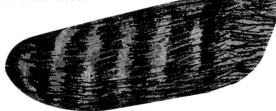

SAGE GROUSE

When preparing for a date, the sage grouse male alters his appearance. He spreads out his twenty tail feathers and inflates two orange sacs in front of his chest until they are as big as tennis balls. Then he struts back and forth, showing off.

The female hen spends about fifteen minutes a day grooming her feathers. The sage grouse male spends TEN TIMES MORE TIME preening himself. How many minutes will he spend grooming?

SLOTH

These good natured animals live in the forests of South America. Sloths will spend all day just hanging upside down from a branch by their three curved toes, eating leaves.

Sloths crawl clumsily and slowly on the ground. When they are being chased they move at least TEN TIMES SLOWER than most people run. If you ran your fastest, you might run one mile in nine minutes. How long would it take a sloth to travel that same mile?

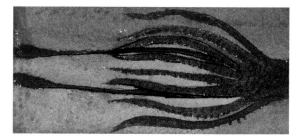

SQUID

Animals that have no backbones are called invertebrates. Giant squids are the heaviest invertebrates alive and they weigh more than three tons. Squids have eight short arms used primarily for swimming and two longer ones for catching fish. A giant squid's eyeball is bigger than your head.

Giant squids can be TEN TIMES LONGER than the tallest basketball players are tall. If a basketball player is seven feet tall, how long would a giant squid be?

STARFISH

If a starfish loses an arm, it may grow a new one. The missing arm, meanwhile, may grow a new body. Now there are two starfish where there used to be only one.

Most starfish have five arms, but some have TEN TIMES MORE. How many arms would a starfish like this have?

TARANTULA

TARANTULAS are giant hairy spiders. Their bodies are bigger than your fist. Like other spiders, they have eight eyes and eight legs. When threatened they rear up on their four hind legs and show their fangs, but they are not aggressive. Some tarantulas can be kept as pets and even walked on leashes. Their bite will kill a small insect instantly but their mild venom is harmless to humans.

Most spiders live less than one year, but both male and female tarantulas don't mature until ten years of age. Males live, at most, one year after they mate. Females who survive predators live TEN TIMES LONGER after mating. How many more years will most females survive?

WILD BOAR, WARTHOG, AND BABIRUSA

These animals are all relatives of the pig. Wild boars were brought from Asia to the United States to be hunted as game animals. Warthogs are African wild pigs and Babirusas are Indonesian.

All males have four long tusks. The two upper tusks (honers) are for digging, and to impress the females. The two razor sharp lower tusks (rippers) are for fighting. A dog might dig three inches to unbury a bone. Wild boars will use their honers to dig TEN TIMES DEEPER for food. How deep do they dig?

ZEBRA

Each zebra has a unique pattern of stripes. These stripes blend in with tall grasses and shadows helping the zebra hide from the hunting lions.

A zebra can run as fast as a racehorse. If you jogged at a steady pace, you might run four miles per hour. A zebra is TEN TIMES FASTER. How fast do zebras (and racehorses) run?

INDEX

ANSWERS

ANT   Five hundred pounds. That's like lifting a full refrigerator all by yourself.

ARMADILLO   Ten feet long. That's the distance from the floor to the rim of the basketball hoop.

BUMBLEBEES   One hundred flowers in ten minutes. Six hundred flowers in one hour. Six thousand flowers in ten hours!

CAMEL   Fifty glasses. That's more than three gallons of water in one minute!

CENTIPEDE   One hundred and twenty feet. That's the distance from the end zone to the forty yard line on a football field.

CHIMPANZEE   One hundred and thirty. That's almost how many different words are in the poetry part of this book.

CROCODILES   Two hundred teeth. That's more teeth than the number of M & M's you eat if you finish two super size bags at the movies.

ELEPHANT   Four hundred pounds. That's like eating 1600 quarter pound burgers every day. That's a ton of food every five days.

FROG   Sixty feet. That's like jumping from home plate to the pitcher's mound.

GIRAFFE   One hundred and ten pounds. That's more than most sixth graders.

GOLDFISH   Twenty inches. That's the length of two open pages of this book.

PEACOCK   Thirty pounds. That's heavier than your biggest backpack stuffed with books.

RACCOON   Eighty. That's as many as the number of musicians in some symphony orchestras.

SAGE GROUSE   150 minutes. That's the time it takes to watch five half hour sitcoms in a row.

SLOTH   Ninety minutes. One and a half hours. That's as long as a world cup soccer match.

SQUID   Seventy feet long. That's as long as a bowling alley.

STARFISH   Fifty arms. That's as many arms as the starting players for both sides of the Superbowl plus the three referees have, all together.

TARANTULA   Ten. That's twenty years from birth to death.

WILD BOAR, WARTHOG, AND BABIRUSA   Thirty inches. That's as deep as the distance from the top of your kitchen table to the floor.

ZEBRA   Forty miles per hour. That's faster than cars drive down your street.